CW00867274

Another Coffee Break Short Stories

and other things

PAM SWAIN

ISBN-13: 9781489534736   PAM SWAIN

DEDICATION

This book is dedicated to my four grandsons, Ethan, Justin, Noah and Max. Also to my children and son and daughter in law. Lisa, Moira, Ben, Graham and Jess. Thanks also for the support and encouragement, as always, from my friends Ann and Trevor.

ANOTHER COFFEE BREAK

ANOTHER COFFEE BREAK

CONTENTS

The Forest Guardian

The cold of the night would soon arrive. We realised the urgency of getting back to our campsite as soon as possible. Having gone looking for firewood in the nearby forest, we had been fooling around so much that we had become lost. Then, the snow started blowing a blizzard.

My younger brother, Ted, had got us into this situation, although my father said it was my fault. Ted, my best mate Russ and I (Dave) were normal teenage boys. We liked to get up to mischief. Shouting abuse and causing trouble made us feel important.

Okay, maybe encouraging Ted to throw eggs at the old guy who used a walking stick, and laughing when he fell over, was going too far. But, hey, I know plenty who have done worse.

Another coffee break

Our father is ex Army, very strict and thought that a suitable punishment was to leave us stranded in this God forsaken place. He left us a tent and supplies for the weekend. He had even taken our phones away. We hated camping, always had, even when Dad had dragged us for a "men's bonding week under canvas."

Nightmare! "It will make men of you," he said," and you can reflect on your behaviour and learn a bit of respect."

Of course, first we had to go and apologise to the old guy and do some chores for him as way of punishment.

We don't have a Mum, she died a year ago and that's when we started misbehaving. Since then Dad just ignored us most of the time and yelled at us the rest, so we had to do something to get his attention. We were growing further and further apart.

"Ouch! Damn!" Ted cried out, as he fell over a root sticking up out of the ground, shaking me away from my thoughts.

"I think I've sprained my ankle," his eyes filled with tears as he tried to balance on his sore foot.

"For goodness sake, man up," I said, sounding like my father. I reached over and put my arm round him, immediately feeling guilty for how I had spoken to him. He was only fifteen after all.

Another coffee break

Helping him across the path, I cleared a space in the snow with my shoe, and we all sat next to each other under a large tree.

"Russ, come with me and help me look for leafy branches to shelter us. And then, guys, I know you don't want to hear this, and we won't tell anyone, but we need to huddle together to keep warm."

Some of the survival skills our father bored us with must have sunk in.

Ted's ankle had swollen so much he needed to remove his boot so Russ and I took our socks off and put them on his foot to try to keep it warm.

"Let's see, what have we got to our advantage?

A pair of fingerless gloves, a scarf, and a woolly hat, and we all have hoods. Zip up your fleeces, pull them up over your face, and pull your hoods down as far as you can. We can use the hat, scarf and gloves for our hands. Between us, we have a Swiss army knife, torch and chewing gum. Not a lot we can do with that," I said, dividing out the gum.

The night set in and we were freezing. Snow fell heavily in flurries around us, and the wind blew it into our faces. I knew it was important to stay awake, I didn't know why, but Dad had said so.

"Maybe now is a good time to think about what we have been doing," I said, knowing if we talked it would keep our minds active.

"Well, it's your fault that we are here so stop acting the big man," my brother growled at me.

Another coffee break

"How do you figure that out? You were the one that knocked the old guy over, smarty," I replied giving him a thump on the arm.

"I just did it for you guys to accept me otherwise you wouldn't let me hang out with you," he said.

I thought about his reply for a while and realised he was right. He looked up to me and did what I told him to get me to acknowledge him. I realised at that moment that I was leading my brother down a slippery slope, and I'd have to be a better role model.

"I think we should keep movement in our bodies. Let's wiggle our toes, then our ankles, knees and so on to keep the circulation going," I mumbled.

"Good idea," Russ said.

"What's that noise?" Ted called out.

The night noises were terrifying, and I had been trying not to draw attention to them. We recognised owls hooting, but it was the unfamiliar noises that frightened us most. We could identify snow falling onto branches, but the scurrying of animals close by made the hair on the back of our necks stand on end. Could there be foxes or animals that were circling us getting ready for the kill? Our minds were in overdrive.

"Maybe its vampires or a chain saw murderer," suggested Ted.

"Don't be daft," I said," that sort of thing only happens in movies." I turned on the torch to give myself reassurance. "It will just be animals settling down for the night."

"Wish I was going to a nice warm bed, even the tent would be OK,"complained Russ.

Another coffee break

"I can't feel my foot, and my ankle is throbbing, and I'm freezing,"moaned Ted.

"I know, we're all freezing," I said, leaning over to rub his numb foot. He screamed in pain when I touched it.

"Not numb now then," I said unkindly, as tears came to his eyes.

"We will be okay, Dave, won't we?" he asked.

"Of course, we'll get out of here in the morning," I said, with more conviction than I felt.

"Look!" called out Russ, "over there. Can you see that flickering light?"

"Yes, yes, I see it. Hey! Hello, over here! Someone must be out looking for us." I said, without thinking it through. No one knew we were here.

"Help! Hey! Over here!" I turned on the torch and shook it from side to side. The flickering light was getting closer and then the torch flickered off.

"You idiot," Ted said to me. "Why didn't you check the batteries? Now they won't find us."

"Yes they will, come on Russ stand up and yell and make noise," I said.

We thumped our frozen feet so hard the pain was intense, at the same time whistling, yelling, and shouting until the flickering light turned towards us.

A young girl, around fourteen or fifteen, wearing just a pair of jeans, Wellington boots, and a light tee shirt, was holding a massive lantern.

"Hello," she said, as if it was the most natural thing in the world to come across three strangers, stranded in the forest, in a snow blizzard.

"I'm Emma. Follow me."Russ and I pulled Ted into a standing position, and each with an arm round him, we followed her.

She walked in silence, and although I fired many questions at her, she remained quiet. She was intent on her mission of getting us to safety.

Our bodies stung from the cold and we found it difficult to keep up with her. Without turning round, she paused now and again, to let us catch up.

Presently we came to a clearing with a wood cabin that had smoke coming from the chimney. It had a porch running along the front and a plaque above the door carved in wood.

I could barely make it out, but as Emma turned on the outside light, I could see it read, "Emma lives here."

Once inside Emma set about looking after us. She gave us blankets, and we sat in front of the roaring fire eating a stew she had prepared earlier. It was a bit creepy because she had three places set already, and three beds made up, as if she had been expecting us.

It seemed strange that a girl this age was living alone in the forest and the way she dressed, on a cold winter night, was odd.

"Was the old man, okay?" Emma asked, in a sweet voice.

"How did you know about that? I asked.

Another coffee break

"You would be surprised how much I know about you," she replied.

"It's time to listen to your father, and learn to respect people. We don't get very long on this earth. We have to do as much as we can to help others," she said. "Treat others as you would like to be treated, and then you can't go wrong."

"You seem to know about us, tell us about you, Emma," I said.

"I'm not very interesting," she said. "I got lost in this forest several years ago, and died of hypothermia. Now I look out for others that are lost, and bring them here when they need help."

"You mean you're a ghost?" I asked.

"Well, I like to call myself a spirit, it sounds less frightening than ghost. I always know when people are stuck in my forest and need help. That is my destiny. I loved helping others when I was alive and chose to continue in death. It is a lovely feeling," she said

"Not a feeling I would know about,' I thought. But maybe I should think about it. It felt good looking after the lads and helping them to stay warm. I didn't admit to them, but I actually enjoyed chopping wood and stacking it for the old guy. Maybe I'll go and see if he needs help with his garden. It looked like it could use it. My mind was listing jobs that he may need done, and I had noticed his neighbour's lawn was a mess. When we got out of here, I was going to take the lads round and do jobs for all the people we had upset. And anyone else that needed it. I guess I've learnt something about respect after all.

We gradually thawed out in front of the fire. Emma helped us get warm by making hot drinks and wrapping us in blankets. She even had fresh, dry clothes warming in front of the fire for us, all a perfect fit. She gently bandaged Ted's ankle, spread some special ointment on it, and fetched a wooden crutch from the corner of the room to help him walk. It was weird but she seemed to know everything we would need, and had it ready.

After stoking the fire, Emma disappeared for the night, and we had a cosy sleep in our freshly made beds. She was back in the morning making breakfast. We woke to the glorious smell of frying bacon, egg and hot chocolate. The fire was roaring in the fireplace, and the hut was warm.

Last night seemed like a bad dream, as we sat round the table eating our breakfast I told the boys of my thoughts. Strangely, they had both had the same ideas as me.

Emma was fussing around us, with a smile on her face, and I realised she had put the ideas into our heads.

She had shown us what acts of kindness could achieve as opposed to the hurt that acts of nastiness can cause.

"That was lovely, thanks, you're a good cook. We're going to chop wood and stack it for you," I said. "It's the least we can do."

"And I'll do the dishes," said Ted, clearing them into the sink. His ankle was back to normal, thanks to whatever Emma had put on it.

Another coffee break

Emma looked pleased and laughed. "It's OK, it all happens by itself. I never have to chop, stack, or do dishes. I put all my strength into helping people, and everything else takes care of itself. Now it's time for me to take you back to your campsite."

As we walked, I found I could talk to Emma with ease. She got me. She understood. Losing Mum was the worst thing that ever happened to me. But she made me realise it hadn't just happened to me, but to my brother and father too.

"So, would your mum be proud of the way you are behaving?" she asked."What would she say to you right now

 I looked at my feet as I spoke. "She'd be disappointed and ashamed of me.

She would tell me that she had not brought me up to act like that. That I was being a bad influence on Ted and should be a good role model for him."

I could just hear her. She would have sat beside me, turned my cheek toward her, and looked me straight in the eye. She always did that when she was telling me off or having a serious conversation with me.

She never raised her voice, but when she was annoyed, she talked firmly, slowly, and her eyes flashed. That got through to me more than being shouted at.

"I'll always love, respect, and remember her but she wouldn't want me taking out my hurt on the world and ruining my own future, and possibly, Ted's too. She had invested too much love and energy into steering us on the right path for me to throw it all away. I know she would have admired you, Emma, and encouraged Ted, and me, to become more like you," I said.

Emma nodded, smiled, and stretched her arm out in front of her in a pointing gesture. There, in x\ |||| front of us, was the campsite, just the way we had left it, except covered in snow.

The three of us ran towards the tents as though it was a long lost friend, and began knocking the snow off. I turned to thank Emma, but she had gone. I ran to the edge of the forest to look for her, but she had disappeared.

As if on cue, a familiar black four-wheel drive pulled up to the other side of the campsite, and my father came towards us.

He said '|I've come to check on you because of the snow."

He had with him a large Thermos flask of piping hot soup. We sat in the car with the engine running, the heater on and we talked properly for the first time since Mum died.

"I should have been more understanding of your feelings, boys. I couldn't connect with you because I was hurting too much. I was trying to block it out. I couldn't bear your hurt as well, so I neglected you both, but it's not going to happen any more. It was very selfish of me.
I've had time to reflect while you've been gone. We can get through this together, we're still a family and it's what your Mum would have wanted," he said, tears filling his eyes.

"You boys are my world, and together we can make the future Mum would have wanted for us." he said.
Mum would have been proud of us. Her teenage sons, and husband, crying out their feelings and

Another coffee break

becoming men.

"Dad, can we go home now, please? There are things we need to do," I asked.

Our lives turned round that day and Russ, Ted and I went on to become strong, loyal, respectful and compassionate men. Our bond was never broken, and we developed a wonderful closeness with Dad.
We helped in our community, and I became a Community Counsellor. Every year, at our old campsite, Ted and I ran a camp for teenagers who were going astray.

We found the clearing where Emma's cabin had been, the only reminder of it was the plaque that says "Emma Lives Here", which we keep at the campsite. And as for Emma, we never saw her again.

<u>The Anniversary Cruise</u>

The cruise ship swayed from side to side as Pat walked around the deck. She breathed in the fresh smell of the sea, and a fine mist of water left a salty taste on her lips. The listing of the ship did not bother her. She was a good traveller, and had never experienced travel sickness.

David was completely different. He finally gave in to her and booked a cruise for their anniversary. He bought just about every seasickness cure known to man, including a bracelet to be worn on pressure points on his wrist.

The decks were gleaming and sparkling clean. As she neared the stern of the ship, she heard muffled cries of laughter, bellowing and splashing.

Another coffee break

She saw children and families playing by the pool. Children stood on the edge of the pool and jumped in, crashing with muffled thuds as they slammed into the water. Some held their noses and jumped, others dived. David would have enjoyed watching them. He loved children, and they had planned to have a large family, but it did not happen.

The lifeguard was having a busy time scrutinizing the crowd carefully and keeping track of the sheer number of people.

Now and again, Pat heard the shrill noise of the whistle when he was trying to get someone's attention

As she walked, she came upon a group of passengers arguing loudly, and shouting at each other in a disagreement over a game of quoits.

They were having a heated discussion over points and were accusing each other of cheating.

Pat walked briskly by, disliking hearing people screaming at each other. She went to the other end of the deck and sat at a table. She chose one with a large parasol for protection from the scorching sun.

A waiter, carrying a white cloth and silver tray, took her order. Her cocktail looked delicious. It was pale pink with a sweet fruity aroma. A small umbrella stuck out of the top and rested against the pinstriped straw.

Chunks of ice, chopped pineapple, and strawberries bounced to the top. She stirred it slowly with the long spoon. It looked frothy, syrupy, and was surprisingly gratifying. It cooled her throat, and she felt it slide down to her stomach. It was so cold it took her breath away.

Another coffee break

But it refreshed and cooled her from the inside out. She sipped it slowly to make it last.

As she sat, she watched large seagulls swooping and soaring high in the sky on the wind. They glided gracefully without moving their wings. They appeared peaceful, and two of them flew together in perfect harmony reminding her of herself and David. Further down, three more were on the ship's rail cawing and flapped their wings at each other, complete opposites of their counterparts.

Pat could feel the burning sensation of the sun shining on the top of her feet. Her sandals didn't give much protection so she reached into her bag and searched for the sun cream. As she rubbed it on her smooth skin it felt silky and had a fragrant scent. She applied it to all her visible parts and sat back and looked round her.

She could not believe David was missing all this. He knew this was a special trip, and that this is what she had always dreamed of. But what he didn't know was that she had just found out days ago that their life dream had come true, and that they were to become parents. The flu she thought she had turned out to be a new life forming inside her. She had not had the chance to tell David, and had kept it for a special announcement over dinner on the cruise.

Life has a way of dealing up the unexpected and David had been taken from her suddenly in a car accident on the way home from work.
She had come on the cruise to put her life back together and to spend time thinking of him.

As she walked back to her promenade deck cabin, she looked up at the giant glimmering ship

Another coffee break

and felt a lump in her throat. Her heart was heavy
as she walked along, then she stopped short.

A white feather came fluttering out of nowhere
and landed at her feet.

David was letting her know he was with her after
all

In the blink of an eye

Wriggling his red swollen toes he felt the hard coldness of his boot soles. A lack of circulation made his painful feet feel of pins and needles. With stiffness spreading up his legs he pulled himself into a sitting position. Taking off the thin blanket he pushed it roughly into his backpack. Then removing a half bottle of water from his bag, he dribbled it onto the palms of his dirty chapped hands and pulled on his fingerless gloves. He let out a deep sigh. Life was not like before. It had changed in a blink of an eye. Feeling twenty years older he rubbed his face with water. His long black hair had a whisper of gray through it.

Another coffee break

He used to be proud of keeping it trim, now it felt itchy and greasy and he wore it in a pony tail with an elastic band.

Wiping his long matted beard and taking a mouthful of water he swilled it round his mouth and teeth. He rubbed his piercing blue eyes and then relieved himself behind some bushes, rinsed his hands and took a deep breath. Time for his day to begin. A different life than before.

Pulling his black beanie over his ears, he shivered with cold and buttoned up his heavily stained jacket and made sure his collar was up round his neck. The colour of his shirt was unrecognisable and his trousers were full of holes and stains.

He rummaged through bins looking for food and found a cheese sandwich, cold chips and pizza slices. Having devoured the sandwich and chips ravenously he carefully placed the pizza in newspaper in his jacket pocket.

People were staring at him and making comments, children were particularly cruel often holding their noses and pointing. If only they had seen him before.

He shuffled up Main Street and ducked down the alleyway to the supermarket car park and peered around to make sure he wasn't being watched.

He climbed onto the side of the food bin and carefully lifted the lid not wanting to be caught and humiliated again.

The stale smell of putrid food filled his nostrils nearly making him wretch. He found some unopened sandwiches before the supermarket manager came running towards him shouting abuse.

He walked quickly away and didn't stop until he got to the war memorial. He sat in his usual spot,

Another coffee break

round the side, on the third step, where he was out of the sight of the main town.

He spread his blanket on the cold stone step, unpacked his goodies and spread out the sandwiches and pizza slices. His mouth watered as he peered at them.

He closed his eyes and remembered a heavily laden table of Christmas dinner, steam rising from the golden skinned turkey, gravy, hot roast potatoes, stuffing, sprouts and carrots and parsnips. He could almost taste it but was interrupted by a noise and opened his eyes, to see a dog grabbing a piece of pizza and running off. He threw a pebble in its direction, not wanting to hit it but it frighten it. Mumbling under his breath he put the food back into his bag and clutched it as if he was expecting the dog to return. He closed his eyes again and thought of his life before.

After a while he heard someone clear their throat nervously and saw a tall thin young man wearing jeans and a black hooded fleece standing above him. The man 's sleeves were rolled up and the end of a tattoo was visible on his arm. He was clean shaven and had striking blue eyes and slightly elongated features. There was a silver loop dangling from his right ear and three silver studs on his left.

The man spoke in a quiet reassuring voice.

"Hi there."

He looked up at the young man and nodded.

"Do you mind if I sit here?" the young man said pointing beside him.

He nodded again pushing his backpack over a bit.

"My name is Si. I'm a journalist. I've seen you here before. Could we have a chat"

Si pulled out a couple of burgers and a bottle of pop.

Another coffee break

"Here, I brought you something." Si said handing him a burger and pop. He savoured every morsel of it and sipped the pop slowly to make the pleasure of it last. It was a long time since he had any. The drink caught the back of his throat and the effervescence, eye watering cold liquid slid down his throat and trickled it's way to his stomach.

They chatted, small talk at first, then Si told him about himself. If he was repulsed by the looks or smell of the homeless man he showed no sign of it. Gradually Si got him to talk about himself.

"My name is Nat," the homeless man said.

Si asked "How come to live like this? I work for an organization that helps the homeless. I want people to know how easily it can happen to anyone."

He thought for a few minutes and then nodded his head.

"I had a good life, before." Nat started. He was surprised to hear his own voice as he hadn't spoken in a long time.

"I had a lovely wife and two wonderful children." He sighed deeply. "We were happy. Then it fell apart, like dominoes, one after the other."

It was a long time since he had let anyone close and it all just spilled out. Nat was wary of telling this stranger his business but as he spoke it felt like therapy. He felt emotional at the unfairness of it all.

"Mel and I met at school when we were 14. We were inseparable from then on. We married and I qualified as a plumber and opened my own business. We bought a three bedroom house. Soon we had a son who we called Anthony, after my father, who had died the previous year. It was bittersweet.

Another coffee break

Mel's parents died in a car accident years before and she was extremely close to mine. She and my mother were best friends. Both of us were only children. Our lives seemed complete when we had our daughter, Jenny."

He paused and took a swig of pop. Si joined him and they sat in silence for a moment. A sadness came over him as he was remembering.

"My mother was visiting us one Sunday, when she collapsed. She passed away before the ambulance got her to hospital. She had a massive heart attack.

The suddenness and shock of it affected us both deeply. I was on autopilot till after the funeral and even then couldn't accept it.

 Slowly we helped each other through and soon Mel discovered she was pregnant again. It seemed like a light in the dark. Mel found this pregnancy especially difficult without mum. We had another little girl who we named Angela. Mel had her by caesarian. A few days later they had been discharged and we all went home. The second day home and Angela was in my arms and when I looked at her and I saw her lips were blue and she was limp. Everything after that seemed to be in slow motion."

Tears rolled down Nat's face, he sat for a few minutes and sobbed into the tissue Si had given him. He blew his nose hard and continued.

"That is when everything became unravelled. Angela had passed away from an undiagnosed heart condition. Mel began drinking and online gambling. She was suffering from post natal depression. The children were seeing a counsellor to help them through and I was struggling to keep everything together.

Another coffee break

Mel was secretly borrowing payday loans to cover her habit. She borrowed more and more to pay for each previous loan. She had given up on the kids and me and the house.

I booked her an appointment with a counsellor but she refused to go. Then one day she just left. I was distraught and contacted the police.

It wasn't long before they found her body. She had jumped off a bridge. Tears streamed down both their faces and Si shook his head and put his arm round the other mans shoulders. They sat in silence for several minutes.

"After that I tried to pay off Mel's debts but I lost the house and car and my business. My kids were taken into care and I became homeless. I tried to find out where they were but no-one would help. I applied for benefits but because I had been self employed I wasn't entitled to anything so that's how I found myself like this."

Si thought for a moment then said,"With your permission I would like to upload your story on45 the internet and make a Go Fund Me page. Come with me and we will get you sorted out."

 Si took Nat to his flat, fed him, let him have a bath and lent him some clean clothes. Then he took him to a hairdresser that cut homeless people's hair for nothing. After a shave and haircut Nat felt better and fell asleep on Si's settee.

Si stayed up late into the night writing his article. By the time he went to bed there were several hundred pounds in the Go Fund Me account.

Nat woke up next morning to the smell of cooking bacon which was making his mouth water. He followed the aroma and he found Si cooking breakfast.

Another coffee break

"Morning Si. Something smells good."

"Good morning Nat, why don't you go have a wash while I get breakfast ready. I have planned a long day for us.

The Go Fund Me page had gone through the roof once Nat's story had come out. Thousands of pounds had rolled in overnight.

Si took Nat to find accommodation and buy clothes and necessities.

After filling his larder and putting away a bit of the money to live on until he got a job, Nat asked for the rest of the money to be used to help the homeless.

With Si's recommendation and Nat's own experience he was given a paid job with the council on a team to help homeless people.

Once he was settled and had a comfortable home he and Si began to search for his children. After several weeks they managed to trace them. They were in a foster home together and were as excited and happy as Nat was to see him again. He visited them every day and it took another few weeks for the paperwork to be completed and they moved in to Nat's house.

They lived very happily together and as a family helped in soup kitchens for the homeless and collecting goodies to take to them. They collected blankets, toiletries, clothes and whatever else was needed and spent some evenings every week delivering them. Nat never forgot his life before and how life can change in a blink of an eye.

LOVE IS

Love is living, love is dying

Love is trusting and relying.

Love is pain and hurts a lot

Love is giving all you've got.

Love is gentle, love is kind

Love is always on your mind.

Love is fun, love is laughter

Love is cherishing and looking after.

Love is holding hands while you walk

Love is giggling and pillow talk.

Love is eyes that look so deep

Love is secrets shared to keep.

Love is not having to pretend

Love is faithful to the end

Love is problems together solved

Love is in each others lives involved

Love is interested in your mate.

Love is going on a date

Love is feeling safe in each others arms

Love is sheltering from harm

Love is hugs, kisses and cuddles

Love is sorting out the muddles.

Love is patience and understanding

Love is tender and not demanding.

Love is so many things

Love is ……………………………..love.

Another coffee break

They had nothing to say to each other.

They had nothing to say to each other. This was the first time in 38 years of being together that there was silence between them. Greta couldn't believe that Bill had left her. They had been so happy and this had hit her hard. How was she going to manage without him? She was angry with him and she was very afraid. Afraid of being alone and sleeping in their bed without the reassurance of his warm arms round her.

As she sat in the chair with a rug pulled up over her she looked out the window at the dark foreboding February sky.

It was snowing heavily and she thought of how they had loved the snow and gone outside and played in it like excited children. They lay next to each other making snow angels. Now it just depressed her looking at it. Her thoughts filled with the past.

They had met when they were both twenty and in college where they had passed several times in the corridor and had shared lectures but it was not until her best friend Dora set them up on a blind date that they actually met each other. They had clicked immediately and from then on were rarely apart.

They knew the first time they kissed that they would spend their lives together. They were married 6 months later and lived in a shabby bedsit together near the campus. Their parents weren't against them being together, just that they felt it was too soon to marry and that they were too young.

Bill had taken on a part time job to pay their rent and they lived on baked beans or soup but they were ecstatically happy. When College finished

Another coffee break

they both got jobs and their parents helped them out with a deposit for a house. They wanted to have a family when they were young but months turned into years and it never happened. The tests showed that it would never be possible.

Greta remembered they cried that night until there were no tears left.

She had brought up the subject of adoption but Bill was not open to it and it broke her heart and that was the only selfish thing he had done in their marriage until now.

They had become each other's world and were able to afford expensive holidays and whatever they liked as they had no one else to worry about. They had promised each other that they would grow old and gray together and it would be a good life. Bill had died. She was angry with him. He had promised.

He had been a wonderful husband until about three months ago when he became difficult to liv with, his mind always seemed to be elsewhere, and he was snappy and not sleeping and unhappy. He was secretive and making and receiving private phone calls at which time he would swiftly leave the room.

He had mysterious outings that he would not share with her and even stayed away overnight without telling her where he had been. It frightened her.

She had never been a jealous wife, never had any reason to be until then. One evening, after one of the phone calls, Bill had gone out to the garden and had left his phone behind. Greta lifted it and quickly looked at the last missed call. "Missed call from Demi," was on the screen. With shaking hands she returned the phone to where he had left it and went to find him. She was trembling all over now and was terrified of what he might tell her but she had to know.

So many thoughts were going through her head and nearly making her crazy. "Was he going through a mid life crisis? Was Demi a young blond 19 year old or was she married too? Did she work with him and see him every day? Or worse of all was he in love with her?"

She found him sitting on their garden bench, with his eyes closed and a troubled look on his face. His eyes were scrunched up and his brow furrowed as it always was when he was deep in thought and worried. He didn't even hear her sit down beside him. Then she noticed it, a solitary tear running down his cheek. Her heart hurt. She wanted to take him in her arms but she was too angry with him.

She sat quietly and after a few minutes gently touched his hand. He opened his eyes and looked at her.

His eyes were red and puffy. She waited for him to speak, it had to come from him, and he had to be ready to tell her. Finally with a shaky voice, it all came tumbling out. It was worse than she thought and she felt her heart break at that moment but she had to be strong and not let him see how much it had hurt her.

She would need the strength and she could break down after he had gone. She wouldn't cry in front of him. He told her he would always love her and that he had not planned for this to happen. It was just one of those things.

She listened quietly and wiped his tears as he repeated over and over how sorry he was. Sorry that it had to happen this way, he had been uncertain for months as to whether he would leave her but the phone call tonight made had confirmed it. He had no choice any more. He had to go. Greta leant forward and placed her hand on the polished wooden coffin in front of her. She intended to stay with him all night just as she had done in the hospital. Tomorrow she would have to say goodbye but she didn't want to think of that just now.

He had fought the cancer as long as he could and Dr Demitrius had tried everything to ease his pain. In the end he had slipped away quietly in his sleep.

 Dr Demitrius or Demi as his patients called him had been treating him for months and for a while it had looked promising which is why he had not worried her about it. He had overnight stays in hospital when he was too ill to come home after treatment.

He assured her that although she wouldn't be able to see him he would always be beside her. She closed her eyes and thanked God for the wonderful gift he had given her of a wonderful happy life with someone who adored her.

She lifted her hand off the coffin and whispered "till we meet again."

A shared moment

Clouds of whitest white

In a sky of deepest blue

Air so clean and fresh.

Among tulip stems

A timid dormouse labours

To ease his hunger.

He gnaws and nibbles

With speed but little movement

An old apple core.

Eyes unblinking, brown

Are soft shining and alert

Hold me in their stare.

Busy all the while
The gentle breeze above him
Sways the tulip heads.

Sunshine warms his back
Apple soothes his hungry needs
Greedily he works.

Across sunlit fur
Lines of shadow pattern slant
Silence rules his world.

Without thought of fear
We hold each other's stare, till
Slowly I move on.

By Sarah Hutchinson (authors late mother)

Another coffee break

<u>Green Tea.....really?</u>

Pip handed Ann and I teabags of green tea. We were at our Healthy Life course and she was telling us how green tea could help with weight loss.... Really? Apparently four cups of it a day would burn off 100 calories. "Does that mean if we ate a biscuit with it the tea will counteract the calories? I asked, tongue in cheek. "Good try," laughed pip "but it doesn't work that way."

Before the class ended Pip asked how many of the twenty five of us drank green tea and only one hand went up. "Hmm" I thought "one out of twenty five isn't exactly an advert for it. "Do you drink it black?" someone asked. "No, you drink it green" someone else answered laughing.

Days later, teabag was still unused. I had smelled it, examined it, looked at it and still hadn't plucked up the courage to try it.

Was Pip trying to get rid of us because we were the mischievous duo of the class? Ann phoned and asked if I had tried it yet. Noooo. She hadn't either. Bet it was going to taste awful. Every time I went to the kitchen I saw it sitting there beside the kettle. I WILL try it before next class....really. Will it make my tongue green? Will it be bitter? Not looking forward to this.
Courage plucked up I went to the kitchen and boiled the kettle. I put the teabag into a cup and waited for the kettle to boil. Just then the phone rang,

Another coffee break

"Oh dear what a pity" I thought "better answer that." I was glad to put off the inevitable for a little bit longer.

Phone call finished, all out of excuses I headed with a heavy heart to re-boil the kettle. I poured boiling water on top of the teabag and left it for a couple of minutes.

With a steaming mug of green tea in front of me I held my nose, took a sip and prepared to spit it out. Swallowed. Hmmm! Not bad. Quite refreshing, sort of tasteless but pleasant. Made me realise I shouldn't judge a teabag by its colour. I wouldn't mind a second cup. I will have to buy some....really

Brothnell Brothers

This won't be much fun, thought Jessica, as she opened the door. Not with the people she worked with. She had started her new job as a data input clerk 6 weeks ago and was already bored senseless. She needed money to pay for her flat since Patrick had moved out 3 months ago leaving her with unpaid bills. She applied for every job but this was the only one she got an interview for. She had been in her dream job corresponding for a fashion magazine and had loved it but the magazine downsized, letting her go.

Jessica had been prepared for the job at Brothnell Brothers to be boring but she hadn't expected the staff to be too. How wrong she had been.

Another coffee break

Mrs Davies was the account clerk. Each morning when Jessica arrived Mrs Davies was already at her large mahogany desk which was facing Jessica's. Mrs Davies was in her late 50s and had worked for Brothnells for 35 years and she was proud to be the longest serving employee in the company.

Her half glasses perched so far down her nose that Jessica wondered how they didn't slide off. Gray showed through her mousy hair which she wore pulled up in a severe bun on the top of he head. Her steely blue eyes seemed to glare at Jessica and made her a little afraid.

She wore little make up and every day she wore the same green tweed suit with a different coloured blouse. Her blouses were high necked and tied with a huge bow which was adorned by a

Celtic design brooch. At break and lunch time Mrs Davies stayed at her desk, methodically took out her lunch box, flask and knitting and sat in a little world of her own.

She was knitting a Christmas jumper for her son. Jessica couldn't help but imagine the dreary Christmas they must have and had visions of a grown up man wearing a home knitted jumper with a reindeer on the front. The thought made her giggle inside. Mrs Davies always seemed to be less grumpy after lunch and occasionally came out with some hilarious comment to the office general and then went silent again.

Pippy, the other data input clerk had red frizzy hair, freckles and was very pretty. She was a little scatty and giggled a lot. She was tall and skinny and was always drinking tea. She had three trousers suits that she wore alternatively. Black, green and blue. She never took her jacket off and wore tight short tops underneath that hugged her figure. Her blue eyes were covered in dark eye shadow that must have taken hours to put on and her face was matted with make up to cover her freckles. She disappeared every lunch time and ran breathlessly back into the office right on time after lunch.

Mac Dawson was the office manager. His desk faced the room. The office setup looked like something out of the fifties.

Mac wore a suit and shirt and tie every day. He wore a different tie each week. Now it was December, he was wearing a Santa tie.

It seemed so out of character, Jessica thought. Mac had a long face and slightly protruding teeth and a well clipped moustache adorned his top lip. His dark hair was thinning and he wore it in a comb over. His black shoes were always immaculately polished.

Ronnie was the office junior/tea boy. He walked with an uninterested gait and was obviously unhappy in his job. His green eyes had no sparkle. Jessica thought he was a good looking boy but he walked around with a scowl on his face and didn't even talk in complete sentences.

He would say,' tea' as a question and also when he placed it on the staffs desk. Invariably he put it down so roughly that it sloshed on to nearby paperwork. He wore black flannel trousers and an open necked shirt and black trainers.

Taylor Green was the head clerk and he wore knitted cardigans and black trousers. He was a handsome man but didn't take care of himself. His eyebrows looked like they were taking over his face, and his hair always seemed badly cut and his clothes were often crumpled.

Another coffee break

The three salesmen at the end of the office, Pete, Dave and Ken, were out of the office most of the time just checking in to do their paperwork.

The other staff kept themselves to themselves and although Jessica saw them in the tearoom at lunchtimes she never felt included so she just read a book.

Every Friday evening the staff met at the local pub, they invited Jessica but she could not think of anything worse than spending time outside the office with them. Tonight she was forced to join them because it was a mandatory Christmas dinner in a private room at the local hotel.

They had been asked to bring a plus one but she had come alone.

As she opened the door she took three deep breaths and put a smile on her face. The long festively decorated table was full. Everyone else was already there and the first thing she heard was the mumbling of conversation and loud laughing and giggles.

At first she thought she had the wrong room. A handsome young man that she had never seen before came forward and said, "so you are Jessica, I have kept you a seat beside me."

Jessica was gobsmacked. Who was he? A lady she didn't immediately recognise spoke: "Jessica this is my son Mike." She recognised the voice first and then in astonishment realised it was Mrs Davies.

Her face was impeccably made up and her hair was flowing round her shoulders, she had put a colour rinse in it to cover the gray. She wore a low cut fitted red dress with a white pattern. It stretched provocatively over her ample bosom. She had a red necklace with matching earrings.

Another coffee break

Jessica sat open mouthed looking round the room. It was like being in the twilight zone.

Taylor Green sat opposite her and introduced her to his wife Milly who was in a wheelchair. Taylor looked dapper tonight in his brown leather jacket and open necked blue shirt although his hair cut was still crooked. Milly's carer had tended to her needs tonight and that left him time to get ready. His usual daily routine was to get Milly ready leaving little time for himself.

Milly had been his hairdresser and although her hands shook he still let her cut his hair.

Pete, Ken and Dave were huddled together at the end of the table. They mumbled together and then roared with laughter as they exchanged jokes. Jessica couldn't believe it when she saw a smartly dressed smiling young man with twinkling eyes. It was Ronnie. He had his arm round Pippy's shoulders and she was gazing lovingly at him.

Jessica realised that Pippy met Ronnie lunchtimes and that is why she disappeared every day.

Her biggest shock was when she realised Mac Dawson was dancing with his wife on the dance floor.

He was boogying and she couldn't believe the tight brown trousers and open necked patterned shirt, he wore cowboy boots and an earring in his left ear! He was wearing a red cowboy hat with tinsel round the rim; it had little lights that flashed on and off.

Crackers pulled, party hats on, jokes exchanged and Christmas Carols being sung. Drinks flowing, good spirits and laughter resounded through the room.

Jessica was trying to comprehend everything when a gentle voice whispered in her ear. It was

Another coffee break

Mike. "I know what you are thinking, I used to work with mum in the office and the only way she could get through it is with the tipple of whiskey in the tea in her flasrefused to go to their nights out, as well, thinking they were stuffy and boring. One night she needed me to drive her and I went in and couldn't believe how different they were. The Brothnell brothers are retired but refuse to modernise and expect their staff to dress in a certain way. They do spot checks to make sure things are still running as they like it.

Jobs are hard to find and the money is good so the staff just put up with it and between them came up with the plan to meet every Friday night so they could be themselves. I go with them now and they are brilliant fun and they have talked about you. I wanted to meet you to see if the same thing applied. "What do you mean?" Jessica asked.

"Well, you have given them the impression that you are uninterested in getting to know them.

They thought you were the boring one, sitting reading your books and hardly speaking to them." Mike said. His hand touched her shoulder and she got a feeling inside that she hadn't felt for a long time.

Jessica smiled. Now she understood. She excused herself and went to the ladies room. She looked at herself in the mirror; she had dressed down to fit in. She wore a black skirt with a plain blue blouse. Putting her handbag on the shelf beside her she pulled out her make-up bag and carefully selected her favourite blue glittery eye shadow, her black mascara and applied her foundation and plum lipstick and sparkly lip gloss. In her bag she found large hoop earrings and a multicoloured scarf that she tied loosely round her neck. Hair loosened, she let it fall in waves round her shoulders.

There was nothing she could do about the sensible flat shoes she was wearing so she slipped them off, put them in her bag and felt much more relaxed in her stocking feet.

Lastly she sprayed herself with perfume. She stood back and admired her work. This was the true Jess, not staid Jessica. This was going to be fun after all, thought Jess, as she opened the door.

Our Tutor asked us to write about a quest but something unusual so here is what I wrote.

Quest???

You re- quest- ed we write about a quest

Which quest, what quest, that is the quest- ion?

I set myself a quest- ionaire to find out

Whether it could be a con- quest, be- quest or in- quest.

Its quest- ionable that it was a con- quest

Unlikely to be a be- quest

So let's have an in- quest into it.

Let's see. I will be the quest- ioner

Into the quest- ion able story of the quest.

Another coffee break

I have re-quest-ed an in-quest into the be-quest of the story of the quest

And as the quest- ionare I re-quest that we forget about quest- ing into

The meaning of quest, the story of quest or even a quest itself.

Because there is no quest- ion that your re- quest is just too hard.

DUNLUCE CASTLE

They walked hand in hand down the path towards
the castle.
The wind howled and the waves crashed loudly
against the rocks below.
The jagged ruins loomed in the dusk
Giving a hauntingly spooky effect under the
gloomy sky.
They stepped back in time through countless
generations
Filled with an eerie excitement.
The ruined walls high above them cast shadows
where they stood.
Filling their imaginations with wonders of the
past.
They sat huddled together on a low wall in the
biting wind.

Another coffee break

Eyes closed, listening….
They shivered as they heard the rough breaking of
the waves

And the whistling of the wind

OR

Was it the ghosts of past times with generations of
voices brought alive in their minds?

What made them shiver they wondered?

Had they felt the pain of those lost souls who had
lived and died here?

Had they stolen uninvited moments of castle life
hundreds of years before?

They opened their eyes and strolled together

Looking around in awe at the beauty of this
magnificent ruin.

There was a kind of sadness about this place.

The corpse of a castle that in days gone by sat in
all its splendor overlooking the sea.

Buzzing with everyday life, a daunting deterrent
to its enemies.

They thought how many thousand people had
stood in this very spot

And they somehow felt intertwined with their
lives.

As they walked away they looked back as if to
imprint it all in their minds

And they knew this would always be their special
place.

About the author

Pam Swain was born and grew up in Northern Ireland. She moved to Sydney, Australia for eighteen years where she gave birth to her three children. She is retired and now lives in Northumberland. Pam is the proud grandmother of four boys. She is the author of a fantasy novel `The Enchanted Kingdom, and Coffee Break Time short stories and Taking a gamble and childrens books Harrison Hedgehogs new shoes, Sukie Tristan and Jeremy Jay, which are available on Amazon.

42057312R00047

Printed in Poland
by Amazon Fulfillment
Poland Sp. z o.o., Wrocław